LITTLE HOUSE

Laura Ingalls Wilder

MY FIRST LITTLE HOUSE BOOKS

DANCE AT GRANDPA'S

ADAPTED FROM THE LITTLE HOUSE BOOKS

By Laura Ingalls Wilder

Illustrated by Renée Graef

HARPERCOLLINS PUBLISHERS

For Rhonda
—R.G.

Weekly Reader is a registered trademark of the Weekly Reader Corporation
2005 Edition
Dance at Grandpa's   Text adapted from Little House *in the Big Woods, copyright 1932, 1960 Little House Heritage Trust*
Illustrations copyright © 1994 by Renée Graef   All rights reserved.
Library of Congress Cataloging-in-Publication Data   Wilder, Laura Ingalls, 1867–1957.   Dance at Grandpa's / adapted from the
Little house books by Laura Ingalls Wilder ; illustrated by Renée Graef.   p.   cm. — (My First Little House books)
Summary: A young pioneer girl and her family attend a wintertime party at her grandparents' house in the Big Woods of Wisconsin.
ISBN 0-06-443372-2 (pbk.)   [1. Frontier and pioneer life—Wisconsin—Fiction.   2. Family life—Wisconsin—Fiction.
3. Parties—Fiction.   4. Wisconsin—Fiction.]   I. Graef, Renée, ill.   II. Title.   III. Series: Wilder, Laura Ingalls, 1867–1957.
My first Little House books.   PZ7.W6461Dan 1994   [E]—dc20 93-24535   CIP   AC   Typography by Christine Kettner ❖
HarperCollins®, 📖®, *and Little House® are trademarks of HarperCollins Publishers Inc.*
Printed in the United States of America

Illustrations for the My First Little House Books are
inspired by the work of Garth Williams with his
permission, which we gratefully acknowledge.

Once upon a time, a little girl named Laura lived in the Big Woods of Wisconsin in a little house made of logs. She lived there with her Pa, her Ma, her big sister Mary, her baby sister Carrie, and their good old bulldog Jack.

One winter morning everyone got up early, for there was going to be a big party at Grandpa's house. While Laura and Mary ate their breakfast, Pa packed his fiddle carefully in its box and put it in the big sled waiting by the gate.

The air was frosty cold, but Laura, Mary, Carrie, and Ma were tucked in snug and warm under robes in the sled. The horses pranced, the sleigh bells rang merrily, and they went off through the Big Woods to Grandpa's house.

It did not seem long before they were sweeping into the clearing at Grandpa's house. Grandma stood at the door smiling and calling them to come in.

Laura loved Grandma's big house. It was fun to run from the fireplace at one end of the big room all the way to Grandma's soft feather bed on the other side.

The whole house smelled good. There were sweet and spicy smells coming from the kitchen, and the smell of hickory logs burning with bright, clear flames in the fireplace.

Before long it was time to get ready for the party. Laura watched while Ma and the aunts made themselves pretty. They combed their long hair and put on their best dresses. Laura thought Ma was the most beautiful of all in her green ruffled dress.

Soon people began to come to the party. They came on foot through the woods with their lanterns, and they came in sleds and wagons. Sleigh bells were jingling all the time.

The big room was filled with tall boots and
swishing skirts, and there were ever so many babies
lying in rows on Grandma's feather bed. Laura
thought Baby Carrie was the prettiest.

Then Pa took out his fiddle and began to play. All the skirts began to swirl and all the boots began to stamp. "Swing your partners!" Pa called.

Laura watched Ma's skirt swaying and her dark head bowing and thought she was the loveliest dancer in the world.

Soon it was time for dinner. The long table was loaded with pumpkin pies, dried-berry pies, and cookies. There was cold boiled pork and salt-rising bread. How sour the pickles were! They all ate until they could eat no more.

The fiddling and dancing went on and on until
it was time for Laura and the other children to go
to bed.

When Laura woke up, it was morning. There were pancakes and maple syrup for breakfast, and then Pa brought the horses and sled to the door.

Pa tucked Laura and Mary and Carrie and Ma into the sled. Grandma and Grandpa stood calling, "Good-by! Good-by!" as they rode away into the Big Woods, going home. What a wonderful party it had been!